∽ The Classic Tale of ∾
Ginger & Pickles

Manufactured in U.S.A.

8   7   6   5   4   3   2   1

ISBN 1-56173-594-9

Cover illustration by Anita Nelson

Book illustrations by Sam Thiewes

Publications International, Ltd.

Once there was a little shop called "Ginger & Pickles." The shop was just the right size for dolls. Lucinda and Jane, who lived in the dollhouse, always bought their groceries at Ginger & Pickles. The counter inside was also just the right height for rabbits.

Ginger & Pickles sold red spotted handkerchiefs, sugar, and galoshes. The shop sold nearly everything, except for a few things you might want in a hurry—like shoelaces, hairpins, and lamb chops.

Ginger and Pickles were the owners of the shop. Ginger was a yellow tomcat and Pickles was a dog.

The rabbits who came into the shop were always a little bit afraid of Pickles. The mice were rather fearful of Ginger. Ginger usually asked Pickles to help the mice, because he said helping the mice made him hungry.

"I cannot bear to see them going out the door carrying their little packages," said Ginger.

"I have the same feeling about rabbits," replied Pickles. "But it would not be right to eat our own customers. They would leave us and go to Tabitha Twitchit's store."

"Actually, they wouldn't shop anywhere any more if that happened," replied Ginger gloomily.

Tabitha Twitchit ran the only other shop in the village. And she did not give credit.

Ginger and Pickles gave unlimited credit.

Now the meaning of "credit" is this: If a customer were to buy a bar of soap, instead of paying for it with money right away, she says she will pay another time. Pickles, being a very kind sort, would make a low bow and say, "With pleasure, madam." Then Pickles carefully writes the amount of owed money in a book. The records for all the items bought on credit were kept in this book.

Customers came again and again, and bought a lot, in spite of being afraid of Ginger and Pickles. Everyone liked to use the credit that Ginger and Pickles let them have. But there was no money in the money drawer. Day in and day out, lots and lots of customers came and went. But they never paid as much as a penny for peppermints!

And as there was never any money, Ginger and Pickles had to eat food from the shop. Pickles ate biscuits and Ginger ate canned fish. They would eat their dinner by candlelight after the shop was closed for the day.

The first of January came around. As Ginger and Pickles looked over their record-keeping books, they realized they still had no money. Poor Pickles was unable to buy a dog license. He was not able to walk about outside without a dog license.

"It is very unpleasant," Pickles told Ginger. "I am afraid of the police."

"It is your own fault for being a dog. Being a cat, *I* do not need a license," replied Ginger.

"I am afraid I will be arrested. I have tried to buy a license on credit at City Hall, but they do not give credit there," said Pickles. "The place is full of police officers, too. I met one as I was coming home."

"Let's send another bill to Samuel Whiskers. He owes us quite a lot for bacon," sighed Ginger.

"Let's send *everyone* their bills again," said Pickles.

Ginger and Pickles went into their room in back of the store. There they worked on the bills. It was quiet as they added up numbers, numbers, numbers.

After a while they heard a noise in the front of the shop. As Ginger and Pickles walked to the front of the store, they were very surprised at what they saw. An envelope was on the counter, and a police officer doll was writing in a notebook! Pickles nearly had a fit. He barked and barked!

"Bite him, Pickles!" called Ginger from behind a sugar barrel. "He's only a doll!"

The police officer doll kept writing in his notebook. Pickles kept on barking and barking until he finally just gave up.

When it was all quiet, Pickles found the shop was empty. The officer had disappeared. But the envelope was still on the counter. Ginger walked over to the counter and picked up the envelope. Pickles was becoming very worried about the whole situation.

"Do you think he has gone to get a real live police officer?" Pickles asked Ginger. "I am afraid the letter says I must go to court."

"No, you do not need to go to court," answered Ginger, who had opened the envelope. After carefully reading the rest of the letter, Ginger announced, "It is a tax bill."

Pickles was upset. They had no money for the things they already needed. Now they were going to have to pay taxes, too. "This is the last straw," said Pickles. "Let's close the shop." So Ginger and Pickles locked the door and shutters, and left. The closing of the shop caused many problems.

Tabitha Twitchit immediately raised the price of everything in her store by a penny. And still she refused to give credit.

Everybody was pleased when Sally Henny-Penny put up posters to say that she was going to reopen Ginger and Pickles' shop. The posters said, "Henny's Grand Opening Sale! Penny's penny prices! Come try, come buy!" The posters made everyone want to visit the new shop.

On opening day the shop was filled with customers.

Sally Henny-Penny gets rather nervous when she tries to count out change, and she does insist on being paid in cash. But she is quite harmless.

And her store has a remarkable assortment of bargains. There is something to please everybody!